Dragon Tales

A BOOK OF DRAGONS
BY JOHN PATIENCE

DERRYDALE BOOKS
New York

Mr Pringle and the Dragon

fter retiring from his job at the paint factory, Mr Pringle became bored and decided to become an odd job man. He wrote out a card and put it in the window of the corner shop. The card read:

Odd Jobs
No job is too big. No job is too small.
Contact: Mr Pringle, 13 Station Road.

The next morning, as Mr Pringle was enjoying a nice cup of tea, his doorbell rang and there, on his doorstep stood his first client! "Good morning," she said politely. "I'm the Witch of Far Away and Long Ago. I saw your card in the shop window and I have a little job for you. It's not much really, just a bothersome dragon that needs slaying in Long Ago. I'd do it myself but I'm busy in Far Away." "Well, dragon-slaying is not exactly my line of work," said Mr Pringle cautiously. He suspected that this might be some

kind of practical joke. "Anyway, shouldn't I have a magic sword to do the slaying with?" "Cats and broomsticks!" cried the Witch. "You're quite right – I've forgotten to bring the sword. Oh well, it can't be helped. You'll have to make do with this." The Witch plucked a long silver pin from her pointed hat and handed it to Mr Pringle. "Here, just a minute," he began. "Sorry, I must be flying," said the Witch. "And so must you. Good luck." And, saying this, she blew at Mr Pringle as you might blow at a dandelion clock.

It was only a little puff of breath, but it blew Mr Pringle right off his feet and clean out of this world. Head over heels he spun, through swirling clouds of rainbow mist. His head was filled with a sound like tinkling wind chimes and he tingled from head to foot. "Stop! Stop!" cried the old man, and quite suddenly everything went still. The mist cleared and he found himself standing in the middle of a beautiful, fairytale city.

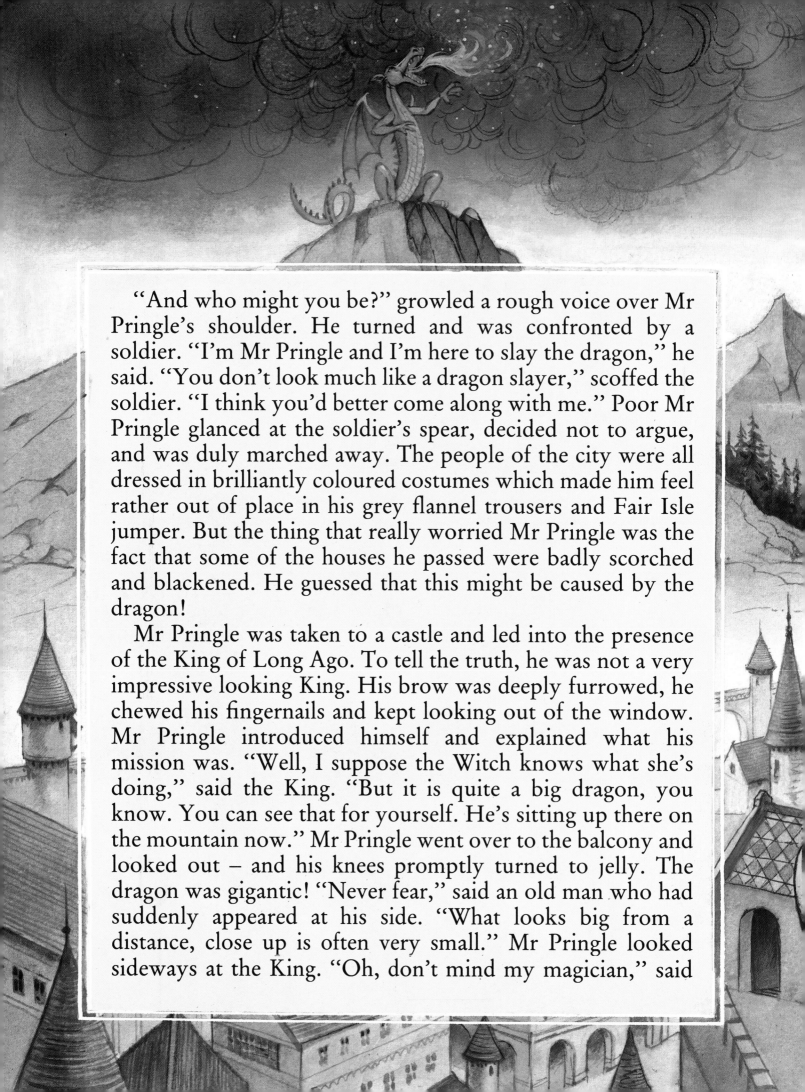

"And who might you be?" growled a rough voice over Mr Pringle's shoulder. He turned and was confronted by a soldier. "I'm Mr Pringle and I'm here to slay the dragon," he said. "You don't look much like a dragon slayer," scoffed the soldier. "I think you'd better come along with me." Poor Mr Pringle glanced at the soldier's spear, decided not to argue, and was duly marched away. The people of the city were all dressed in brilliantly coloured costumes which made him feel rather out of place in his grey flannel trousers and Fair Isle jumper. But the thing that really worried Mr Pringle was the fact that some of the houses he passed were badly scorched and blackened. He guessed that this might be caused by the dragon!

Mr Pringle was taken to a castle and led into the presence of the King of Long Ago. To tell the truth, he was not a very impressive looking King. His brow was deeply furrowed, he chewed his fingernails and kept looking out of the window. Mr Pringle introduced himself and explained what his mission was. "Well, I suppose the Witch knows what she's doing," said the King. "But it is quite a big dragon, you know. You can see that for yourself. He's sitting up there on the mountain now." Mr Pringle went over to the balcony and looked out – and his knees promptly turned to jelly. The dragon was gigantic! "Never fear," said an old man who had suddenly appeared at his side. "What looks big from a distance, close up is often very small." Mr Pringle looked sideways at the King. "Oh, don't mind my magician," said the King. "He's always saying things like that. I think they're supposed to make him sound wise, the way proper magicians do in fairytales. He isn't magic at all really."

Some time later, up on the mountain top, the dragon narrowed his cruel, yellow eyes, and watched a tiny, balding figure walk out through the city gates, pick his way across the wasteland between the city and the mountain, and begin to climb. The figure was Mr Pringle.

Though he was very frightened he had decided that he could not allow himself to be defeated by the first odd job that came his way. It could be very bad for his reputation! Mr Pringle climbed and climbed and at last, there he stood, trembling before the enormous, monstrous, fearsome, terrible, beasticalburbulating, fire-breathing foe! "What do you want?" hissed the dragon. "Well, actually, I've come to slay you," replied Mr Pringle. "But I don't much like violence. I'll tell you what, why don't you just fly away like a good dragon and save all the nastiness?" The dragon laughed. A great horrible laugh it was, that sounded like the bubbling of a volcano. "No! I'll tell YOU what," he roared. "Just for fun, we'll play by fairytale rules; you ask me three riddles and if I can't guess them I'll fly away. If I do guess them, I'll eat you up. How's that?" "Alright," agreed Mr Pringle. "I've got one for you: What's white and swings through the jungle?" The dragon puffed a few smoke rings and thought for a while. "I don't know," he admitted, sulkily. "A meringue-utang," said Mr Pringle. "Here's the second one: What's black and white and red all over?" Again, the dragon paused for thought. "I don't know," he growled at last. "A newspaper," said Mr Pringle. "Now here's the last one: What's long, bent and yellow and travels at ninety miles an hour?" "I don't know," roared the dragon at the top of his terrible voice. "A jet-propelled banana!" cried Mr Pringle triumphantly. "I win. Now off you go, bye bye." "Rubbish!" snapped the dragon, snatching Mr Pringle up in one of his fearsome great claws. "Those weren't proper riddles – they were only jokes. I'm going to eat you up." Mr Pringle wished hard at that moment that he had a magic sword, but instead he found only the Witch's hat pin. Desperately, he plunged it into the end of the dragon's

nose. "Take that!" he cried. There was a loud bang, a shower of coloured sparks, and Mr Pringle was sent flying head over heels. He was spinning back through the swirling rainbow coloured mists with which he had become acquainted at the start of his adventure. But instead of the sound of the wind chimes in his ears, he heard a voice saying, over and over again, "Letter for you, Mr Pringle. Letter for you, Mr Pringle."

Shortly he came to his senses and discovered himself to be standing back on his own doorstep. In front of him was the postman. "Letter for you, Mr Pringle," he was saying. Mr Pringle took the letter absentmindedly. Had it all been a dream? Yes, it must have been. Shaking his head, he opened the letter and found a cheque inside it, for ONE THOUSAND GOLD COINS. The old man gasped. It was signed by the Witch of Long Ago and Far Away and on the back of it was scribbled, "For the slaying of one bothersome dragon."

The Fearsome Dragon

Underneath the mountain,
In his dark and gloomy lair,
Lurks a fearsome dragon.
Go see him if you dare.
I popped in only yesterday,
Cross my heart and hope to die.
I don't go in for stories
And you know I wouldn't lie.
He's horrible and slimy,
And he's coiled up on his hoard
Of silver, gold and precious stones
And you'd think that he'd get bored,
'Cause he wouldn't spend a bit of it
On lollipops or sweets.
He wouldn't touch your candy.
I can't imagine what he eats.
But there's bones that lie all round him
And I thought I saw a cap
That belonged to Billy Bamber –
Do you recall the little chap?
I haven't seen him lately,
He doesn't come out to play.
Perhaps he's got a cold,
Or maybe moved away?
Now about that fierce dragon,
He's there all on his own.
He's got no friends to speak of
And he isn't on the 'phone.
I'm sure that he gets lonely.
Do drop in and say hello.
Does the way your head is shaking
Mean to say that you won't go?

The Enchanted Rock

There was once a dragon who flew down and settled upon an enchanted rock and was turned immediately to stone. The rain and the snow fell upon him, the wind lashed around him and the sun beat down upon his scaly head, but he never blinked an eyelid. One by one, the years passed and a great city grew up around the stone dragon. The people of the city supposed that he was nothing more than a statue, but he watched everything that happened. He saw how unhappy the people were becoming. He listened to them talking, complaining that they had no money because King Skinflint taxed them so harshly that their children were starving and went without shoes. And if anyone had looked closely at the dragon they would have seen tears welling up in his stone eyes and trickling down his cheeks, because inside his great stone body the dragon had a heart as soft as a marshmallow and he felt sorry for the poor people.

Then one morning, as the sun rose, a wisp of smoke curled up from the dragon's nostrils. Slowly, he moved his head from side to side, stretched out his wings and came alive again. A thousand years had passed and that's as long as even the strongest magic lasts. Now the dragon was free he decided that it was high time things were put right in the city, so he flew to King Skinflint's castle. The King was in his counting house, counting out his money when in flew the dragon. It gave him such a fright that he knocked over all his nice, neat piles of gold coins. "Help! I'm being attacked by a dragon," screamed the King. The door burst open and in

rushed a group of guards, armed with swords and spears. "There's no need for all this," said the dragon. "I'm sure we can both be reasonable." "What do you mean?" said King Skinflint gruffly. "Explain yourself quickly. Time is money. That's one gold coin you've cost me already!" "Well you know your subjects are all starving," explained the dragon. "I think you should stop taxing them. You have plenty of gold already – your counting house is full of it." "Don't be stupid!" shrieked the King, his eyes almost popping out of his head. "I need all the gold I can get. Anyway, money is too good for poor people." As he said this the King suddenly

noticed that the dragon himself was covered from head to tail with beautiful, golden scales. "Seize the dragon!" yelled the King. "He's worth a fortune!" Now of course the dragon could have easily flown away, but that would not have helped the poor people of the city. He could have roasted the soldiers and the King to a crisp with his fiery breath, but he was such a gentle creature that he couldn't bring himself to do it. Instead he allowed himself to be captured.

At first the King was at a loss to know what to do with the dragon. Though he was covered with gold scales you couldn't exactly pile them up and count them, like gold coins. Then he had a wonderful idea: other kings rode around in golden carriages, but he would outshine them all by riding upon a golden dragon! And so it was. King Skinflint had a beautiful jewelled saddle made for the dragon and flew upon him all around the city. There was only one little problem with all this as far as the King was concerned and that was that he was small and the dragon was tall. It was nothing really – it simply meant that someone had to give him a leg up when he mounted the dragon. As I say, nothing at all really.

King Skinflint could not have been happier. Though he could see wherever he went that his subjects were impoverished and sad, he didn't mind a jot. In fact he found it all very jolly and would often command the dragon to fly low so that he could make faces at people and shout rude remarks at them. From time to time King Skinflint would fly off to visit other kings, and they would always be green with envy. This made

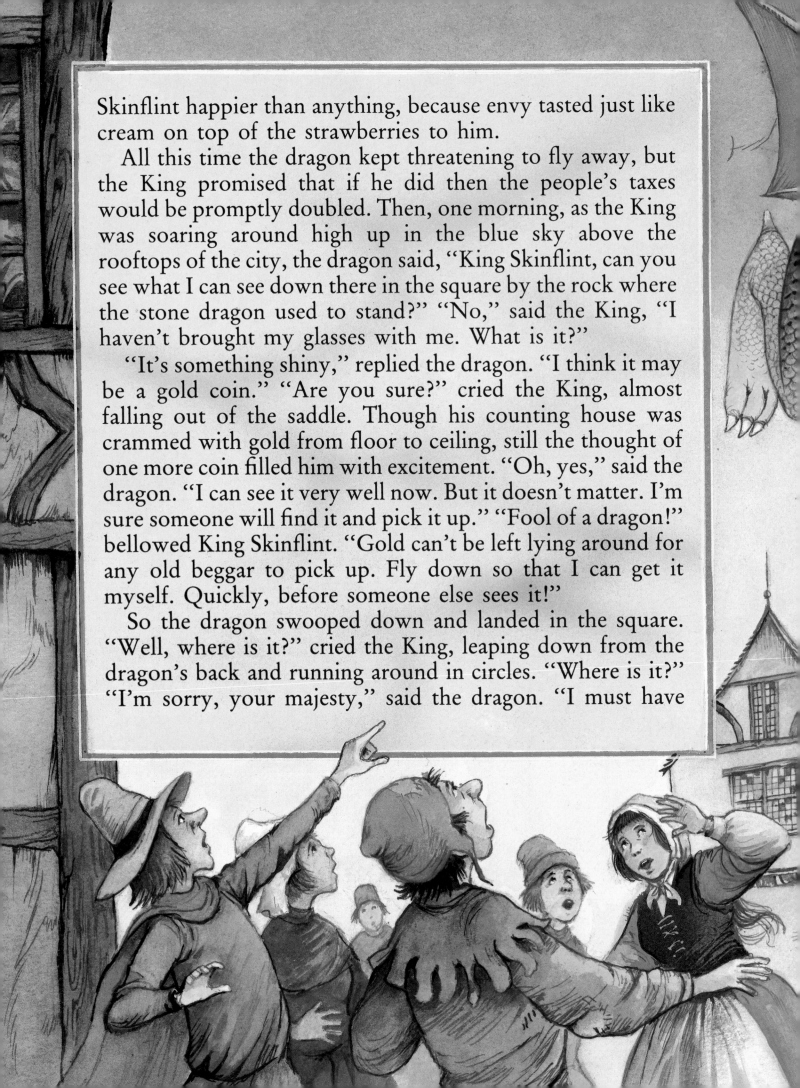

Skinflint happier than anything, because envy tasted just like cream on top of the strawberries to him.

All this time the dragon kept threatening to fly away, but the King promised that if he did then the people's taxes would be promptly doubled. Then, one morning, as the King was soaring around high up in the blue sky above the rooftops of the city, the dragon said, "King Skinflint, can you see what I can see down there in the square by the rock where the stone dragon used to stand?" "No," said the King, "I haven't brought my glasses with me. What is it?"

"It's something shiny," replied the dragon. "I think it may be a gold coin." "Are you sure?" cried the King, almost falling out of the saddle. Though his counting house was crammed with gold from floor to ceiling, still the thought of one more coin filled him with excitement. "Oh, yes," said the dragon. "I can see it very well now. But it doesn't matter. I'm sure someone will find it and pick it up." "Fool of a dragon!" bellowed King Skinflint. "Gold can't be left lying around for any old beggar to pick up. Fly down so that I can get it myself. Quickly, before someone else sees it!"

So the dragon swooped down and landed in the square. "Well, where is it?" cried the King, leaping down from the dragon's back and running around in circles. "Where is it?" "I'm sorry, your majesty," said the dragon. "I must have

been mistaken. Perhaps it was just a piece of broken glass catching the sunlight." "Idiot!" roared the King. "Take me back to the palace at once. I wish to count my money again to cheer myself up." "Very well, climb on my back," said the dragon. The King looked around for someone to give him a leg up, but no-one offered to help. Why should they? He had never helped them. "I'll teach you all," shouted King Skinflint. "I'll triple your taxes tomorrow!" "Perhaps you could climb up on that rock," suggested the dragon, "and hop on my back from there." "Very well," replied the King. He was not used to climbing but needs must, so, huffing and puffing, he struggled up the enchanted rock and, standing on top, he immediately turned to stone. He could not move a muscle, nor bat an eyelid, nor speak a word. "Don't worry," said the dragon. "The enchantment will wear off in a thousand years. That will give you lots of time to think about how greedy you have been."

Then the dragon beat his great wings and rose up into the air. In a little while he was back in the King's counting house. There he picked up a sack of gold and away he flew with it, down the city streets, showering down gold coins wherever he went. All day long he flew back and forth between the counting house and the city streets until at last all the King's gold had been given back to the people. From that day on, no-one was ever poor in the city again and, believe it or not, the dragon was made King!

My Pet

The annual competition
For the most interesting pet,
Was held upon the village green
And judged by the local Vet.
There were cats and dogs
And guinea pigs
And hamsters by the score.
There were parrots, rabbits and goldfish
(Which are really quite a bore).
Tadpoles in jars and spiders from Mars
(At least, Tom said they were),
A pony and a donkey,
A goat and something rare.
A pelican pinched the third prize,
And a python squeezed in second,
But my pet won the first prize,
'Cause everybody reckoned
He's the best pet that there ever was,
A thing that's seldom seen.
He's a great big scary dragon,
All scaly, weird and green!

Where have all the Dragons gone

There was once a dragon called Embers who lived in a cave by the deep, green sea. Every day a little boy would come to play with him and every night the sea would sing him a lullaby. And Embers was very happy.

Then one evening after the little boy, whose name was Joseph, had gone home, Embers lay down in his cave to sleep, and the sea began to sing its song. But this time the song was different:

"Hunt high and low and you won't find a one,
all of the dragons but Embers are gone.
Search far and wide, they're vanished away,
like mist in the morning, like a lost summer's day.
No fiery breath, no scaly green face,
the dragons have flown and left not a trace.
Hunt high and low
and you won't find a one,
all of the dragons
but Embers are gone."

The song made Embers feel very sad. He decided that he must leave his cave and sail away to search the world until he found another dragon. Joseph was sorry to see his friend go, but he stood on the shore, waved goodbye and wished him luck.

For a year and a day Embers sailed away, then one bright morning he saw a mermaid sitting on a rock. She was combing her long golden hair and looking at herself in a mirror. "Have you seen any dragons?" enquired Embers. "Of course not!" replied the mermaid. "Dragons don't exist. They are entirely mythical." "I'm not mythical," said Embers angrily, puffing smoke. "Then you're not a dragon," retorted the mermaid and, diving down from the rock, she disappeared into the sea with hardly a splash.

A few days later Embers sighted land and drifted into
shore on a narrow beach. On the other side grew a deep
forest. Since he had nothing better to do he decided to
explore. He had not gone far when he came upon a unicorn.
It was standing quite still by a pool, looking down into the
water. "Hello," said Embers. "Have you seen any dragons
around here?" "No, I'm afraid not," said the unicorn. "But
come and look into the pool." Embers stood by the unicorn's
side and looked into the water. He saw the reflection of the
tall, tangled trees, but of himself and the unicorn there was no
sign. "Makes you wonder, doesn't it?" said the unicorn. Just
then there was a sound like thunder and a knight on
horseback crashed through the trees. The unicorn disappeared in the twinkling of a thingummybob and left the
dragon to face his foe alone. "At last!" cried the knight. "A
real, live dragon to fight. Now I can prove my bravery to

Princess Prudence. Prepare to fight, dragon!" But Embers was an extremely peaceful creature and had no intention of fighting. As the terrible knight lowered his lance and charged, Embers fled and it was the fastest fleeing you ever saw!

Under the sun and under the moon Embers sailed steadily on until at last he came within sight of another shore. And there, on the beach, he found a gryphon. He was building a marvellous sandcastle. "There's no need to tell me," said the

gryphon. "I know the tide will come in and wash it away, but there is so much lovely sand on the beach and I can't think of anything else to do with it, can you?" "No, I suppose not," said Embers. "By the way, have you seen any dragons lately?" "I believe there's a dragon that lives in a cave over there," said the gryphon, pointing out across the sea with his spade.

Embers ___ the gryphon and, filled with excitement, he sailed ___ re long he came upon the cave. It looked very far ___, and so it should. It was his own home. Poor Embers could have cried with disappointment, but there, in the mouth of the cave, he saw his friend, the little boy.

"Did you find any dragons?" asked Joseph. "No," sighed Embers. "It seems I'm the only dragon in the world." "Never mind," said Joseph. "Do you know, I think I'm the only Joseph in the world?" The dragon smiled. "Let's play monsters," he said. "I'll chase you." "Great!" shouted Joseph and away he ran across the sands with Embers chasing after him.